MY BROTHER IS YUCKY!

Mail to PO BOX 245

Creswell NC 27928

ISBN: 9780578266961

Printed in the United States of America

Published by

DoodleFina Adventure Press

Written by Renee Hodges

Book design by Hollie Lyn Hewitt

Please visit our website at doodlefina.com

"Do unto others and you would have them do unto you"
Matthew 7:12

This book is dedicated to my grandbabies:

Awbry, every once and a while be YUCKY too! AND Brothers aren't THAT bad!

Brody, enjoy every YUCKY minute because it's the best part of being a kid. AND give sissy a break every once in a while!

And to my Yucky Brother Donovan Ruth aka Buddy: MAYBE you aren't as yucky as you used to be and MAYBE you weren't THAT bad. And then again...
Thank you for always being my BIG baby brother and one of my heroes.

My brother is yucky.
He's absolutely gross!
He has ketchup on his T-shirt
and he likes to pick his nose.
His hair is a mess
and his fingernails are dirty.

WHY couldn't he be a girl
and be nice, clean, and pretty?

But instead he's loud.
He's mean to girls and rude.
And he burps A LOT
when he's finished eating his food.

There are holes in his pants
and his shoes are untied.
And I have never, not once,
seen my little brother cry.

There are creatures in his pockets
and mud on his face.

Why couldn't he be a girl
and wear dresses, ribbons, and lace?

But OH NOOO!

He had to be a boy.

I had to get a brother.

I think it's time to send him back.

I'll go and talk to mother!

I'm going to put him in a box
and ship him from here to there!
I'll go and tell mother.
I doubt she even cares.

But Mother says NO!
She'd miss him a whole whole
bunch.

WHAT!? That's not fair!
This is just too much!

But he did fix my bike.
And he shared his ice cream.

And sometimes I get to pick
the cartoons on TV.

He does pick on me
and he can be really mean.
But boy, oh boy! Nobody
better ever mess with me!

And he's really kind of cute
when he finally falls asleep.
So, I guess, this little brother
I'm going to keep.

But my next little brother
had better be a girl:
Or I'll send him right back!
And THAT is my final word!

"Brother and Sister,
Together as Friends,
Ready to Face,
Whatever life Sends."

Robert Brault

About the Author

Renee Hodges

Renee was born and raised on the Outer Banks of North Carolina. She's proud to be from a long line of commercial fishermen and some of the first Coast Guardsmen of the OBX, from both the Scarborough and Beacham sides of her family. Since she was very young, she's found adventures in books and stories. Reading is still one of her greatest joys. She loved telling her four boys all kinds of stories and they have encouraged her to share them. Her hope is that her books will inspire young imaginations, provide a few giggles, and inspire a joy for books.

About the Illustrator

Hollie Hewitt

Hollie Lyn Hewitt is a native of Creswell, NC and has a passion for all animals, especially those that need rescue. Her home is full of fur babies that she either has rescued or is fostering. She has actively volunteered for the Red Wolf Coalition, and it holds a special place in her heart. Hollie shared a love of art from a young age with her older sister, Ashley, and is locally known for her talent. She enjoys all mediums of art and is looking forward to illustrating the books in the DoodleFina collection. When she's not doing art, she enjoys watching anime and reading manga. Hollie believes in being your own person and being true to yourself, as well as expressing love for your passions. She is excited to bring her art to a young audience and looks forward to sharing her talent with them. Hollie has a favorite quote, and it's one she's chosen to live by and encourages others to do the same. "Whatever you imagine can come true" by the artist Wendy Moten on the album The Pagemaster.

CPSIA information can be obtained
at www.ICGtesting.com
Printed in the USA
BVHW021145020822
643617BV00002B/26